Published by ZoeBooks

Printed in the United States of America by

SunGraphics, LLC

ISBN: 978-0-9988357-0-9

To Matt, Mary
+ Oliver

with love

Aunt Patty

2017

Zoe the Short-Necked Giraffe

By Gwendolyn Ryder Poindexter
Illustrated by Pat Rees

For Malcolm and Jeremy with Love

Zoe was a short-necked giraffe living on the plains of Botswana. She was a delightful giraffe and made friends easily. In fact, all of the animals loved Zoe and thought of her as the very best of friends.

That's because Zoe was kind-hearted and always thought about how she could help others. Like, when Rosie the rhino wanted to try some of the sweetest fruits hanging down from a low branch, Zoe reached up stretching her short neck out as far as she could and got some succulent fruit for Rosie.

But Zoe didn't like herself at all. She hated her short neck. All the other giraffes on the plains have long, beautiful, flowing, graceful necks, Zoe thought. Even her little sister and brother had beautiful, normal-sized necks. Why couldn't she have been born with a long, beautiful, flowing, graceful neck like all the other giraffes?

She asked her best friend Gloria, another giraffe – but one with a regular-sized, perfectly normal, long neck – what she thought of Zoe's neck.

"Oh, Zoe," she said, "Nobody cares whether you have a long old neck or not. Everybody loves you. Besides, it can be fun to be different," laughed Gloria as she galloped away.

That's easy for her to say, thought Zoe.

Zoe had often asked her mother whether she thought her neck would grow. But her mother only replied, "I don't think so dear. You have what you have. But we all love you just the way you are. Anything different and you wouldn't be our Zoe."

Zoe's Mom gave her a hug but Zoe couldn't be consoled. Every time she went to the water hole, she looked down and saw her reflection in the water and closed her eyes, hoping that the next time she looked, she would have the long, beautiful, flowing, graceful neck that she dreamed of.

One day, when Zoe and her giraffe friends were playing a game of tag, the giraffes heard a roaring sound. They looked up to see an airplane in the sky and thousands of white papers falling to the ground. Zoe read one of the flyers which said that a new zoo was opening up in the nearby town and they wanted all the people and tourists to see the new animals. Zoe thought the zoo must have an animal doctor there to help keep all the animals healthy. Zoe thought she would go find this new zoo. Maybe the animal doctor could make her neck grow!

Zoe went to sleep that night dreaming of finding the zoo doctor and seeing herself with a long, beautiful, flowing, graceful neck, galloping across the plains.

The next morning, she got up very early and left two notes: one to her parents and the other to her best friend, Gloria. She told them that she was going to a place to get her neck fixed. She told them not to worry and that she would be back soon.

Zoe traveled long and far across the plains looking for the town where the zoo was. Soon she began to get very thirsty and very tired. She was far from home and didn't know where all the water holes were. Soon, she was so tired and thirsty she couldn't go another step and she collapsed on the ground.

When she awoke, a man was putting water next to her in a large metal tub. She drank thirstily and then looked at the man.

"Thank you, kind sir," said Zoe.

"You're welcome, little giraffe," said the man. "What are you doing way out here all by yourself?"

"I'm trying to get to the zoo to see the animal doctor so he can fix my neck," said Zoe. "It's too short."

"It *is* rather short, for a giraffe," said the man. "Come with me. I'll take you there so you can see the zoo doctor."

So off they went. Zoe was so excited. I'm finally going to get a long, beautiful, flowing, graceful neck, she thought. My true, dream neck – the one I should have been born with. I can't wait to show it off to Mom and Dad and my friends. They'll be so happy for me!

After a short drive, they reached the gates of the zoo and drove inside. The man got out of the truck and began talking to another man, who looked at Zoe, smiling broadly.

"Are you the zoo doctor?" asked Zoe.

"Sure am," said the man.

"Can you fix my neck?" asked Zoe.

"Why, I think so, but it may take some time. Why don't you stay with us a while and see what we can do?" said the man.

Zoe agreed and allowed herself to be placed in the pen with the other zoo giraffes and the man closed the gate behind her. Zoe figured on staying for a few days and then galloping home to show off her new, long, beautiful, flowing, graceful neck to her friends and parents. Zoe fell asleep dreaming happily about being at home.

Over the next few days, however, the zoo doctor never came. Instead, lots of people would come every day to look at the giraffes, especially Zoe. They thought Zoe was the sweetest and cutest giraffe ever.

One day, a little boy's hat fell into the pen and Zoe reached down, picked it up, reached over the fence, and plopped it right back on the boy's head! "I love you Zoe," said the boy softly.

None of the other giraffes paid any attention to the people and Zoe became everybody's favorite. Everyone wanted to see "Zoe the Short-Necked Giraffe!"

But after a week had passed with no visit from the zoo doctor, Zoe began to get worried. She asked the other giraffes when the zoo doctor would come to fix her neck so she could go home. The other giraffes told her that there was no zoo doctor and now that Zoe was the main attraction, she was here to stay. Zoe became very sad and began to cry.

Meanwhile, Zoe's parents and friends were frantic with worry. They had looked all over for Zoe but couldn't find her. They couldn't believe that Zoe would actually try to get her neck fixed, but it appeared that she had. But they had no idea where she had gone! One day, while Gloria and the other giraffes were eating some leaves from the acacia trees, an airplane roared overhead and little white papers again fell from the sky. Gloria picked up one and read it:

"Come see Zoe, the only short-necked giraffe in all of Africa," the flyer said.

Gloria told the other giraffes about the flyer and they gathered up all the animal friends and decided to go to the zoo to bring back Zoe. So Gloria, Max the mouse, Manny the monkey and Rosie the rhino began the long trek to rescue Zoe. Manny filled packs of water and tied them across Rosie's back so they could travel all day and night without having to stop at the water holes.

At midnight two days later, they arrived at the locked gates of the zoo. There was no moon out yet so it was very dark.

"How will we get in?" whispered Gloria.

Max slipped through the bars and said "I'll be right back. Go hide by those rocks until I get back." And off scampered Max before the others could say a word. A short time later, Max returned dragging some keys in his mouth and gave them to Manny to open the gates. When the gates were open, they all slipped in and went looking for Zoe.

They passed the lions cages, the penguins and the polar bears and finally saw the giraffe pen. When they found Zoe they (quietly!) shouted with glee. Zoe couldn't believe her eyes when she saw them.

"Come on," said Gloria, as Manny opened the gates. "We're going home." Zoe galloped towards the gates but just as she got close, she saw the zookeepers running toward them.

"Oh, what will we do now?" squeaked Max in fear. Rosie took charge. And that's just what she did. She charrrrggged toward the zookeepers who took one look at the charging rhino and scattered in all directions. Laughing, Zoe and her friends ran through the gates and headed for home.

The first thing Zoe did when she got home was run straight to her parents, and brother and sister!

"Oh, Zoe," her parents said, giving her lots and lots of hugs. "We were so worried about you! We didn't know where you had gone, and we can't believe your friends saved you. Thank you so much everybody."

Once Zoe was home, surrounded by her friends and family who loved her just the way she was, Zoe knew she would never want to be anything but herself again. And as she drank water from the water hole and gazed at her reflection, she realized that she had a pretty ok, long enough, beautiful, flowing, graceful neck after all.